SCHOLASTIC
Phonics

My Perfect Pet

Published in the UK by Scholastic Education, 2022
Scholastic Distribution Centre, Bosworth Avenue, Tournament Fields, Warwick, CV34 6UQ
Scholastic Ireland, 89E Lagan Road, Dublin Industrial Estate, Glasnevin, Dublin, D11 HP5F

SCHOLASTIC and associated logos are trademarks and/or registered trademarks of Scholastic Inc.
www.scholastic.co.uk
© 2022 Scholastic Limited
1 2 3 4 5 6 7 8 9   2 3 4 5 6 7 8 9 0 1

Printed by Ashford Colour Press
The book is made of materials from well-managed, FSC-certified forests
and other controlled sources.

A CIP catalogue record for this book is available from the British Library.

ISBN 978-0702-30906-9

Every effort has been made to trace copyright holders for the works reproduced in this publication,
and the publishers apologise for any inadvertent omissions.

Author
Rachel Russ
Editorial team
Rachel Morgan, Vicki Yates, Abbie Rushton, Liz Evans
Design team
Dipa Mistry, Justin Hoffmann, Andrea Lewis, We Are Grace
Illustrations
Izzy Evans/The Bright Agency

Help your child to read!

This book practises words with more than one consonant next to each other, plus long vowel sounds (like '**br**ight' or '**tr**ee').
Read these words with your child:

starts slurp brown perfect

Your child may need help to read these common tricky words:

my he when me to I'm there one
the of are go be what like I love

Before reading
- Look at the cover picture and read the title together. Read the back cover blurb to your child.
- Ask your child: *Do you think dogs make good pets? Why or why not?*

During reading
- If your child gets stuck on a word, remind them to sound it out and then blend the sounds to read the word: s-t-r-ee-t, street.
- If they are still stuck, show them how to read the word.
- Enjoy looking at the pictures together. Pause to talk about the story.

After reading
- Ask your child: *How is Snoop more like a cat than a dog?*
- *When does Snoop remember he is a dog?*

Can you spot the guinea pig on 6 pages?

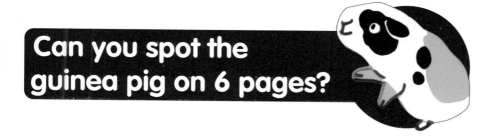

Snoop is my perfect pet dog.
He has soft brown fur.
When he sees me, his tail starts to wag.

But I'm afraid there is one problem.

Snoop thinks he is a cat.

When the rest of the dogs are asleep, Snoop prowls the streets.

When the rest of the dogs are having fun, Snoop naps in the bright sunlight.

Snoop can go up a tree, right to the top!

8

But when he gets stuck, it can be hard to explain what he is doing up there.

Snoop purrs like a cat. He never growls or barks like a dog.

purr, purr

I never see him slurp
his drink or drool.

Snoop grooms his fur and keeps
himself spotless and smart.

One thing is clear.

When it comes to dinner,
Snoop forgets he is a cat.
Then he remembers he is a dog.

I am not complaining. I love my pet dog.

Snoop is a star!

Retell the story